Disclaimer: This is a work of fiction. Names, characters, businesses, places, events and incidents are products of the author's imagination or used in a fictitious manner. Any resemblance to real people, living or dead, or real events is purely coincidental. (Novels, stories).

Illustration and Cover Graphic Design by
Anani Cabrera-Espinal
Editing and Interior Design: Elizabeth Espinal
English Translation and Edition: a collaboration between
Karee Bravo, Anani Cabrera-Espinal & Elizabeth Espinal

Also by

Elizabeth Espinal

Entre Dos Reyes

Aromê

Legend of a Talented Perfumer

Elizabeth Espinal

Dedicated to:

All the young and talented people who dare to dream, breaking the barriers of shyness, and believe that nothing is impossible. Those who dare to have faith. Especially **Luis Arturo** and **Anani**.

To my mom, **Luz Hernandez**, who I want to see smiling with satisfaction.

Thank You, Lord Jesus

For God is the One working in me, both to will and to do His good pleasure.

Chapter 1

A Talented Perfume Maker

Once upon a time, there was a magical meadow, where hills and valleys are loaded with colors. The grass grows and dances to the beat of the wind. The same wind who steals puffs of perfume from the flowers, then spreads it all through the meadow, thus creating a unique aromatic extravaganza in the environment. It's said that this is the work of fairies who spend all spring sealing each flower with their distinct perfume. It's also said that these fairies grant a special talent to some people so that they can grasp the scents more intensely than others. Like a musician, who forms a melody, then makes it come out of his instrument. Only that, a scent is something that is perceived and can paint moments in one's mind. It's for this reason that the birds wake up singing.

When dawn breaks and the first rays of sun awake the day, the scents of grass and flowers begin to rise. The wind is tenuous and different essences start to mingle with magnificent measures, resulting in a unique, fresh, and ephemeral perfume. At that magical moment, I united myself to him. We extend our arms, letting ourselves become enveloped by the atmosphere. We raise our noses high to catch the elusive air, taking soft and deep breaths, holding it in, as if we're transforming into jars that are filled with the aroma of dew. The Master and I remain silent to allow the speech of the daisies, the wings of birds, the wet earth, and the kiss of the sun.

It's my favorite moment of the day, but to enjoy it, I must escape without being seen, so that no one prevents me. The Master and I are accomplices in this. I follow him throughout the valley, chasing variations of aromas brought by the air until they are dispersed by the heat of the day. "Grass and fresh, sweetened ground." He whispered, sensing my presence, and giving a name to the feeling. I closed my eyes to concentrate all my senses. "Honey and Daisies," I replied, about feeling the buzz of the bees, to prove my knowledge. But in opening my eyes I saw him in the distance next to the lake. The delicate mist already began to wane and with it, our treasures.

"There is a big difference between smell and aroma, did you know that?" The Master asked me. "Smells can be good or unpleasant; they are perceived as a part of the raw material. While an aroma is always pleasant, you can perceive them and even taste them with your palate."

"Like fermented cheese?" I asked.

"That's right! You can perceive it by smelling it, and at the same time taste it. It's the same with wine, once it's in your mouth you perceive the smell of the grapes, and all their properties, making the enjoyment of the flavor even more intense..." I loved to show him that I understood him; I knew exactly what he was talking about. Knowing that I had this in common with my father yielded an indescribable joy. Therefore, I wanted to be like him by mastering the art of perfumery. Everyone called him Master Perfumer; his passion for fragrances was such that he knew many different techniques to extract perfumes, with which he created magical, exquisite, and desirable essences. In his workshop, he elaborated balms, candles, incense, and scented soap, but the most intense perfumes were the oils. A couple of droplets and others would immediately notice your presence by perceiving the trace of smell when you passed by. And this is not a common thing, but a rather expensive luxury.

"Aromê! Are you out in your pajamas again?" My maidservant yells. It was common for me to get caught, and scolded for not behaving with the propriety of a lady. After breakfast, they exhausted me with singing and music lessons, to then spend endless hours doing boring embroidery. While Florian—my brother, two years older than me—had as an imposition, the right to inherit the trade, something he didn't particularly enjoy. Florian and I would give anything to exchange obligations. He loves music and instruments, and I long to know all the secrets of the extraction and mixture of liquids in the perfumery. For this very reason, I became an expert in escapes, thanks to my friend Emilien, who constantly came to my rescue. Together we would sneak into the meadow, and he is the one with whom I shared the theories behind my experiments of perfumery. Often we played, describing scents.

"Congratulations, you managed to create a smell worse than pigs. Surely not even dogs will want to get close to whoever wears your perfumes." Emilién said mocking me.

In the same way that we found pleasant smells on our farm, we also discovered foul odors around us. Such as the stench of the stables, for example, and that is only one of many. If you look around, a lot of things smell bad, like the rotten fruits in the markets and the manure left by the horses of the carriages.

"Just as there is incense, there is also smoke." Says the Master. "In a garden, you can find the perfume of roses or the putrid odor of a dead animal. But, it's the bad odors emanating from people, the reason why I'm a perfumer. It is more pleasant to live with someone who smells good than to have to hold one's breath in front of someone who stinks."

How I laughed when he said this, remembering that day when I pointed out the sweaty arms of a worker and said; "That smells bad."

He then pointed to the mouth of a yawning person, who had just woken up and said, "That smells very bad."

It's for that reason that everyone in our house has the privilege of being some of the few who smell good. Even our servants are the envy of the locals, ever since they were awarded toilet cosmetics. However, the perfumes we used were strictly handled by my mother.

Chapter 2

The Perfumer's Trip

*O*ne day my father announced his departure. Convinced that he needed to find new essences to create different perfumes, he embarked to Asia, on a journey that would last for many months. In his absence, new perfumers appeared, but none with the talent and the originality of the Master. Some even tried to bribe our workers to get his formulas. The need to protect the workshop meticulously gave me the opportunity I longed for. Soon my brother, Florian, began to entrust the work to me. In the absence of my father, everyone thought that the son of the perfumer was the apprentice of the master. But among us, it was I who mastered the secrets of the art of perfumery.

Two long winters passed, and the absence of the Master Perfumer became increasingly difficult. We consoled ourselves with the letters that arrived, telling us of exotic places, loaded with promises. I missed him intensely. When spring came, every morning, I ran to the meadow, stretched out my arms, and lifted my nose so that the aromas I perceived would revive his presence in my memory. I managed to magically connect with him for a moment. Sometimes I even heard his voice. "These aromatic powders keep your body fresh all day." I longed to show him how much I knew and to amaze him with the experiments I had made, many of which I sprayed on Emilien to test what they were good for. Thus, I discovered that some poisons of wild berries cause itching and that others, of a sweeter type, attract insects. And I even created odors that made the animals run away. I kept all these a secret to reveal them only to my father.

One morning, after buying spices at the market, we noticed the arrival of an unusually large caravan. Then one of the carriages stopped in front of us. My mother maintained her composure while we all tried to satisfy the same curiosity of the others present. The door opened, revealing an exquisite scent that I didn't recognize, and behind it, emerged the smiling face of the Master Perfumer.

"Father!" I screamed frantically, hurrying to hug him. Part of his greeting was to sprinkle each of us with a different perfume. Citrus and flowers for my mother, contained in an elaborate bottle with crystals and ivory. The perfume he sprinkled on my brother, Florian, had a stout smell, similar to the one he had. But as he approached me, he took out a delicate glass jar, adorned with stones, which hung from a chain. Once open, he waved it in front of my face, letting me perceive the essence.

"Fresh dew and wildflowers," I said, recognizing its likeness to our morning adventures.

"Youthful and charming, like you, my beautiful Aromê. How you have grown! I almost did not recognize you."

"I missed you so much, father!"

"I'm back!" Then, turning to the crowd, he said loudly; "I brought exotic perfumes, cosmetics to beautify the face, creams, and ointments worthy of royalty!"

By that time a multitude had crowded around us, which became the perfect opportunity for the Master to use my mother as a canvas. With the help of a small brush, he distributed an intense red color on her lips, arousing the admiration of all. Also, he accentuated in pink, the cheeks of a pale woman he chose from the crowd. He then approached a distinguished gentleman, asked for his handkerchief, and sprayed it with an aphrodisiacal scent, revealing that it possessed the powers to make the man irresistible to women. After such an exhibition, his fame spread throughout the region, not knowing that it would also arouse envy, causing serious problems.

Chapter 3

The King's Perfume

The news of exclusive fragrances and exotic perfumes brought from distant lands reached the ears of the royals. And for that reason, my father was invited to the palace to grant the King the privilege of choosing for himself the perfume that pleased him the most. Such fragrance would be forbidden for any other person to use. That's how the whole family was invited to the palace.

At the entrance, I was dazzled by the immense gardens. There were flowers everywhere. Some said that these gardens were magical, because they changed forms, creating a different landscape every day, to the delight of the King. Upon our arrival, they moved us into a great hall, where we should wait, since only my parents would be called before the presence of the Monarch.

That's how my brother and I found ourselves surrounded by a crowd of strangers in the waiting room. Luckily for him, there were all sorts of musical instruments there, and he was granted permission to delight the bored crowd. Meanwhile, I was looking for an opportunity to escape into the garden.

I took advantage of the distraction of the guards, to slip out of the room then I scurried down some hallways. Shortly after I came to an area that led to multiple exits. Not knowing which one to take, I hastened to flee for the one at my right hand. Behind me, I felt someone approaching. I could hear their footsteps and I did not want to be discovered. Finally, I burst into a courtyard, guided by the smell of lavender present in the air. I soon found myself surrounded by a beautiful purple garden. Thousands of gardening pots, all identical in size and shape, were lined up, creating structures in an intricate floral maze. "That's how they do it!" I said as I discovered the "magical source." It was still morning, and in the distance, gardeners worked by moving pots, creating new shapes and color mixtures. My curiosity led me to cross a wall, behind which you could hear voices...

"That sword is the one your father chose for you, Your Highness." The officer explained to the elder of the Princes. I realized that I was witnessing the moment when the Princes were being instructed by their officers.

"I want to use that one." Said the Prince, pointing to the sword that was in the hands of his younger brother, Prince Damien.

"Again with the same nonsense, Bastier?" Damien asked, visibly annoyed. "Are we going to rival about my sword or train to defeat our enemies?"

"The practice is going to start when I get what I want!" Bastier replied emphatically.

It was amazing, and at the same time fun to discover such behavior in the royal family. The rumors defining Prince Bastier as a capricious child who always wanted what his brother had, turned out to be true. They talked about how different their personalities were. Damien was popular among the people and took his royal duties seriously. On the other hand, it was said that Bastier, despite being the first in line to inherit the throne, was living in the shadow of his brother, and did nothing to hide his envy. Unable to hold back my laughter, I hid so I would not be discovered. Being there without an invitation would be interpreted as an act of insubordination, exposing me to serious consequences. Silently, I retrieved through the garden returning the same way I came, to go back into the palace. But just as I was leaving the lavender garden, I was surprised-

"Prince Damien!" I said, in fear, bowing before him.

"What do we have here, a lost courtesan or maybe a spy?"

"Oh no, Your Highness!" I replied without looking at his face. "I was only admiring the gardens..."

"What is that smell?" He asked, looking for the aroma with his head.

"Lavender!" I said, pointing to the flowers.

"No, no-no! I have been among these gardens long enough to be immune to their smell. It's a different aroma, a little fresher," he said. As his face got closer to my head, I heard him inhaling through his nose. He was sniffing me! I stood motionless, petrified rather, thinking of what he would do to me and what consequences would my misconduct bring?

"Your Highness, if I may, I would like to apologize-"

"Did you steal that perfume from the flowers? Oh, for sure!" he gasped. "That's what you are doing here! I've discovered an enchantress of flowers!"

I lifted my face, confused, not knowing what to say. Such a statement could become somehow convenient for me. But, if I agreed I would have to prove it and if I denied it, I would be accused of being a spy. "If only my dad were here!" I wished to myself. Then it occurred to me to tell the prince about him. "In fact-" But by that time his squire and one of his officers came to meet him.

"Timeo come. I'll show you something I've never seen before," he said before the officer could inquire about me. "I'll introduce you to... Sorry, miss, what's your name?"

"Aromê, Your Highness!" I said, which seemed to amuse him.

"I knew it! You are the Fairy of Perfumes! You have come to distribute your scent to every flower in the palace gardens, and it has become late... You must be exhausted!"

"That's right, Your Highness!" I said, taking advantage of the exit he provided for me, "...and I'd better leave before my powers disappear!" After bowing, I ran towards the palace. My heart was beating fast, but not from the exercise. I was terrified at the thought of the guard chasing after me and exposing me. In a rush, I entered the same corridors as before, arriving in the waiting room, which by then was practically empty. This made two things obvious: My arrival and my brother's absence.

Then officers approached me, indicating that I should follow them. At that moment, I realized that I had been discovered, and would inevitably face the consequences. I was then taken to a great hall where they announced my entrance before the King.

"Aromê, there you are!" said my mother's voice, to my relief. Confused still, I was reunited with my family. And as I was being introduced to royalty, as the Master Perfumer's daughter, Prince Damien also made his entrance, turning all attention to him, which freed me once again...

"Father, did you call me?" he said as he entered with ease, causing weariness to his brother.

"I hope I have not interrupted an important adventure!" remarked the King, noting the Prince's delay.

"As a matter of fact, Father, today I had an encounter with a mystical being of magical proportions." While he said that, he stared at me, causing my face to blush.

"We will have time for fables later; now I want you to meet the Master Perfumer and his family, who has just been appointed by the Court as Official Master in charge of establishing a School in the Arts of Perfumery and Cosmetics."

"I think it's a great idea, father, another example of your wisdom."

Feeling ignored, Bastier interrupts, "Apart from you, father, does the Master have a perfume for me?"

"That is the reason I asked for both of you. He just came from a long journey, loaded with new and exotic fragrances from which you can choose your favorite."

At that, my father was invited to exhibit his options before the Princes. He displayed several bottles, explaining that the strongest fragrances denoted masculinity, while the floral ones were reserved for more feminine tastes. On the table, each jar had a sample of its ingredients. My father wiped knobs and handkerchiefs so they could smell the scents. Bastier sniffed the handkerchiefs but did not choose, seeming to deliberately delay his decision. Damien, for his part, expressed more enthusiasm. The side of the table next to me contained the feminine perfumes. Damien took the knobs to smell them. After recognizing the fragrance that I carried, he hid it under some handkerchiefs, so that it would not be discovered by his brother.

"Your secret is safe with me..." He whispered. Then he lifted one of the floral scents and said "I like this one! I choose this perfume for myself." Trying to correct him, I shook my head slightly, but he winked at me and smiled, as a signal to stop. At that very moment, his brother wanted to know the aroma.

"As the eldest son of the Princes, I am in my right to choose first," Bastier said.

"Why I'm such a fool, of course..." Damien said, retreating to let him choose. Bastier pretended to be interested in other aromas until he perceived the one chosen by Damien.

"Well, I have already chosen, and I choose this one." He then said carrying the bottle.

My father was going to persuade him to choose another perfume, but I made a noise as if clearing my throat, to stop him. In that, Damien pretended to be dissatisfied, which delighted his brother. Again at the table, my father offers the handkerchiefs for him to choose.

"What is your favorite Madame?" He asked my mother. She indicated that either of them lived up to his dignity. Then, walking towards me he let me choose. Bastier was amused that his brother was willing to use a perfume chosen by a young woman, and with that, he lost all interest in its fragrance. As a result, from that point on, Bastier would smell like flowers, while Damien would wear a bold and

vibrant perfume. A reflection of his personality.

Chapter 4

A Traitor in the Court

The new assignment of the master perfumer brought admiration but also jealousy. In a short time, he was in charge of a school, and the King assigned places in which fruits, spices, and the necessary flowers would grow. In this way, many enrolled as students to learn the trade, and new fragrances were created, allowing both courtiers and foreigners, or anyone who could pay, have access to perfumes and cosmetics.

Because of this, my father acquired good fame and fortune; and as expected, he traveled a lot. Nevertheless, the formulas of their original perfumes remained secret, and those used by the members of the Royal family remained exclusive.

There was a certain member of the royal court, Duke Du Virgile, the King's brother, who like Bastier, was consumed by jealousy and yearned with all his being to rule the kingdom. He had requested a private meeting with my father, in which he demanded to get a perfume equal in body and scent to that of the King, claiming that as his brother, he had the concession to enjoy the same privileges as the monarch. Gripped by loyalty to the king and his principles, my father refused, and instead suggested to the

Duke he would create an exclusive perfume for him. Enraged, the Duke threatened my father.

Henceforth, various attempts to steal from the school labs soon began to occur, and at night in our home too. That's how books with my notes disappeared. They also stole essential oils and flavored waters, which I had created, but they did not find the royal perfumes. Because, once my father saw in me the same passion that he felt for perfumes, he gave me the privilege of having my own workshop. My days at our ranch ceased to be conventional, according to the customs imposed upon a young lady. Once I fulfilled my duties, I spent the rest of the day experimenting and perfecting the techniques that the master taught me, with the help of my friend Emilien. And like my father, I also learned to protect the product of my work. I was able to grow my own flowers, and he even gave me seeds that he had brought from distant lands.

What no one knew was that upon returning from this long journey, knowing that what he possessed was unique and valuable, my father built secret passages that connected our house with an adjacent property. On the outside, it seemed abandoned. But inside, only Florian, Didier, his trusted servant, and I had access. Our most treasured ingredients were stored there, and that was where the exclusive perfumes were mixed. So when they attacked the greenhouse of our garden, thinking that they would leave my father devoid of ingredients, in fact, what they destroyed were some of my experiments.

"But who would do this Father, and why?" I asked, looking with regret at my broken possessions.

"Thieves, my daughter. Motivated by envy." He said with a somber expression on his face. "...and they will not stop until they find what they are looking for."

"I'll help you pick and replant." Emilien offered.

The Master knew who orchestrated this. Duke Du Virgile was an unscrupulous man whose misdeeds he managed to conceal with his power in the crown. And now, with the King on the verge of death, my father knew it was only a matter of time before he had to confront him face to face. Fearing for our safety, he acquired a property in La Provence, hundreds of miles away on the Blue Coast, which he kept secret. There he had daffodils, roses, jasmines, nards, frangipani, orange blossom, and even more exotic species brought from his travels.

In the palace, the health of the King declined more and more, while the rivalry between Bastier and Damien increased.

"If it depended on the people, Damien would be elected as the new king," Emilien said, who came to tell me the news he heard in the town square, about the King and his condition. And he was right... Damien was admired, respected by all, and it wasn't a secret that he was also the King's favorite, but it was also true that the throne rightfully belonged to Bastier. Taking advantage of his weakness of character, Duke Du Virgile convinced Bastier that he was his ally and that he would guard his interests when Bastier came to possess the crown. Hence, the Duke did everything in his power to divide the brothers. He often fabricated stories, making Bastier believe that Damien was the author of conspiracies against him.

The constant arguments among the Princes convinced the King that he should do something in life to ensure that the kingdom was not lost in divisions and wars. He knew that Bastier, once king, would use all his power to annul Damien. He also knew from the shortcomings of his character that he would be an unjust king, that he would take capricious and inconvenient actions. Hence, after consulting with his ministers and the royal laws, he decided to divide the kingdom between his two sons, assigning them lands and duties. He gave Bastier the largest portion of the kingdom, three-quarters of all lands near the palace would be his, while the remaining quarter would correspond to Damien, establishing for him a small kingdom. This time Bastier did not protest; it was a distant land, with rebel groups creating conflicts, with no great palaces as his own, nor an established court. Damien would have to build his kingdom, while he remained in possession of the best part.

The one who was not satisfied, of course, was the Duke. If the kingdom could be divided he also wanted a portion for himself. In this way, he would have the title of a king, even if it was territorial, which would be a beginning, to later concentrate his efforts on eliminating the other Kings becoming the absolute monarch. But his brother, the King, had not taken him into account, so he proposed that he would do whatever was necessary to advance his brother's

death, and then he would go after the Princes.

Chapter 5

The Death of the King

*M*y encounter with Prince Damien had been an amusing experience, which I inevitably remembered often. Either by self-will or because Emilien kept mentioning it, he constantly reminded me of everything that could have happened to me for spying on the Princes.

"You would be preparing potions with mold and rat tails in the palace dungeons," he said, mocking me.

"Maybe I'll make that potion and call it Emilien's Extract. I'll sprinkle it on you in the middle of the square so that all the people will run away from you!" I said, letting out my annoyance.

"In the best-case scenario, they would have you working, planting flower pots in the garden. That would be very convenient for you to see your Prince the rescuer again."

"You make fun of me because you're jealous!"

"Me? Jealous? Of what?"

"That I have been to the palace and you have not."

It was typical of us to bother each other with jokes. After all, that's what friends are for. But, the truth is, it had been nearly two years, and for sure, Damien had already forgotten the whole thing.

"It would be almost impossible for our paths to cross again, especially if the King dies," I explained to Emilien. "Each Prince would assume his role in the kingdom, Bastier would be crowned King, while Damien would go to rule the portion of the kingdom that his envious brother will let him have, or so I think. My father will have to give the royal perfume to Bastier. At least, he will stop smelling like flowers..." (Giggles). By then I knew exactly how to compose each perfume, and it gave me some degree of satisfaction and contentment to know that the jar Damien now used had been prepared by me.

In my reconstructed greenhouse, to amuse myself, I experimented with herbs and all sorts of wild fruits. I came to generate concentrated pungent fragrances, for which my father gave me the nickname of "La Mouffette" (The Skunk). So many times at home I was the object of jokes for being a human skunk. On one occasion, by way of accident, some of my mysterious substances were mixed, generating a thick white smoke, filling the greenhouse with a dense fog. Thinking it was burning, they ran to help me, but I emerged with a jar in my hands to show them my discovery. Didier said that I was a virtuous alchemist. My mother thought I had created clouds. Though it worried my brother when Emilien said it was a magic potion that makes you disappear. "No one should see this," Florian said in dismay. "They could accuse you of being a witch."

"Witch, alchemist, skunk, and creator of clouds," each time they would add more nicknames to the long list of things they called me. However, they needed to add a couple more: "Flower Enchantress" and, my favorite, "The Fairy of Perfumes."

That afternoon we received the visit of some delegates from the palace. "The Master Perfumer is required; he has been ordered to bring incense and ointments to alleviate the sufferings of the King."

With this, we learned that the condition of his highness was serious. Immediately, Didier and my father collected jars, odor powders, candles, aromatic oils, and anything else that would make the King's bed more comfortable. Once in the palace, on the way to the royal chambers, he met the Duke—who promptly warned him: "Make sure you make the last moments of the King as pleasant as possible. Or you will have proven that the title of Master Royal Perfumer is too great to suit you." My father, wary of a trap, requested that two of the most distinguished ministers and the doctor of the court pass with him and observe him. Also, he warned Didier, "If something happens to me, promise me that you will take care of my family." The faithful servant—the only one who knew all of my father's secrets, even those hidden from his own family—promptly replied: "You have all my support and loyalty, Master."

A perfumer not only knows about perfumes but also poisons. It is a must to know what each substance does and avoid those that are dangerous. That is why my father shuddered after seeing the King. He had dark spots in his hands and it was obvious what it meant. Someone was poisoning him! His doctor was talking to Duke Du Virgile, and my father understood that this truth should be revealed to someone else and not to them. It was obvious that there was a conspiracy, but how to know who else was involved and who was not? If only he could talk to the Princes. But then again, would they be getting rid of their father? One thing was certain, the severity of the spots revealed that it was too late to save the King.

The King's room smelled of ointments and incense. They also had lamps with fragrance oils and candles. My father was preparing to retire when he saw Prince Damien, who immediately inquired about the condition of the King, came to his father's bed, took hold of his hand, and consoled him, convincing the Master that, at least, Damien truly loved his father.

He waited until his Highness the Prince came out of the room, to leave. The inquisitive look that the Duke Du Virgile gave him, along with the doctor's indifferent attitude, convinced the Master of his suspicions. On the stairs, at the end of the royal chamber, he found Damien, who did not hide his sadness. After exchanging a greeting with him, he devised a plan to warn Damien as to what he knew without it being obvious.

"The open field and the fresh air are good counselors when the soul feels trapped, Your Highness," he said as advice.

"Thank you, Master, but I do not think I'll find a valid distraction right now," Damien replied.

"Perhaps seeing your father's legacy, in person, will encourage you, Your Highness."

"What do you have in mind?"

"Why don't you visit the perfume school this afternoon? Great progress has been made and I am sure Your Highness will want to see with your own eyes what is happening in the kingdom."

Then Damien, understanding the message said between the lines indicated that he would arrive that same afternoon. Accompanied by Timeo, his trusted officer, and his archer, Damien went through the school fascinated with the progress and satisfied with the economic benefit that this added to the kingdom. Once in the laboratory, the Master Perfumer also took the opportunity to show him the odors by which hazardous substances are recognized. "The process of poisoning is gradual, but there are two ways of identifying it, through the smell of the sick person and..." Extending a medical notes book, he showed him a sketched hand and other drawings indicating the visible effects of the presence of poison.

Seeing this, Damien recognized the spots in his father's hands. He also understood that the call to perfume the King's room was a means of concealing the aroma of the poison. Running immediately to the palace, he informed his brother Bastier. Both then ran to their father's room. There, Damien demanded to smell every bottle of medicine that was supplied to his father, finding in one of them the same aroma that the Master Perfumer had shown him. Enraged, Damien demanded explanations, asking that both the doctor and anyone with access to the King is questioned. The commotion reached the ears of Duke Du Virgile, who hurried to arrive before his name was also in question. Frightened by what the doctor might say, he tried to manipulate the facts.

"A plot to kill the King; that's absurd! Who could do such a thing?"

"That's precisely what I'm going to find out," Damien said, indicating that the doctor, who by then was being treated as a prisoner, should be brought forth.

The visibly frightened man was brought before the court of ministers and councilors, who demanded an explanation. Other doctors had also been brought in to testify to the evidence both in the King's body and in the jar found in his chamber. When it was determined that, apart from this doctor, no one else medicated the King, and that at his request, the Master Perfumer was called to aromatize his rooms, he was accused and condemned to death.

Knowing he was caught, the doctor ran towards Duke Du Virgile to ask for his help, but before he could say anything, the Duke stopped him by slapping him. "You have trespassed my trust and betrayed us all by poisoning our King, and yet you dare to ask for my help? Prepare the gallows immediately!"

"No, no! Duke, tell them, please tell them, please!" shouted the doctor as he was dragged by the guards.

"Duke, what is it that he wants you to say?" Damien asked suspiciously. But before he could inquire further, a guard arrived with the news that the King had passed away.

To prepare the body of the King, apart from the doctors and embalmers, the Master Perfumer was also called. Duke Du Virgile learned of Damien's visit to the perfume school, understanding that everything that happened afterward was due to his encounter with my father. He had long planned to accuse my father of treason, to seize all his property, for the presumptuous Duke was ruined. Now he had another reason to hate him, for having put him at risk of having his plot to seize the kingdom discovered. Seeing the treatment given to him by Prince Damien, he vowed revenge by eliminating them both. "You two are next!"

Chapter 6

Another Encounter in the Garden

Delegates from all over the kingdom came to the palace to pay their respects. These were days of much commotion and changes. They solemnized the funeral of the King, and later they would celebrate the coronations of Bastier as the King's successor and Damien as the King of the Blue Coast. Due to the long ranks of courtiers who came to pay their respects, the funeral ceremonies were extended by a week. Our family attended every day, to help my father in his services. We were given the privilege of using secret entrances by which to get into the palace. With the funeral now passed, I grew tired of staying in that boring waiting room; I used my well-known passages to go to the garden. Remembering the first time I was there, I imagined that, like me, Damien must be exhausted and at the same time very sad. If he loved his father as I do mine, I could only imagine the pain he felt. I advanced to the area where I saw the Princes practicing the first time. To tell the truth, I did not expect to find them there, I was more certain that they would not be, for now, that the funeral was over, my father told us that the brothers were preparing for the coronation ceremony. Another thing he said, and that caused me great anguish, was that Damien would soon leave for his new kingdom, going away forever.

The sound of metal crashing into each other interrupted my pace. I could also hear the swordsmen grunting at the struggle. Who could they be? I wondered, frightened, knowing it could not be Damien. Is this a practice of his soldiers or real combat? I dismissed the first thing by remembering that all the soldiers were called to their posts during the festivities. Not taking another step I remained motionless. It was happening again; "...you got back into trouble Aromê!" I reproached myself, looking for the way to leave without being seen. Then a loud shout shook me, and then the combatants were in front of me, one being knocked down and the other, an enraged victor, stuck his sword on the ground within inches of his opponent. They were Damien and on the ground, his officer Timeo.

"Calm down, Your Highness!" Yelled Timeo.

Damien was breathing heavily; the officer's words compelled him to stop and also to calm down. Getting up, he reached out to Timeo to pick him up, after which both men noticed my presence. I bowed down in reverence, muted and petrified.

Looking at me thoroughly, he asked, "Do I know you?"

"We met once, Your Highness, right here, in this place..."

"The Fairy of Perfumes." He said to my surprise.

"Your Highness remembers me?" I asked with enthusiasm...

"I remember a girl, but what I see now is rather different."

"Your Highness speaks with eloquence and seems to guess my thoughts," I said, letting him see that I thought the same of him. His youthful appearance had changed, the image I kept in my mind of his person was being replaced by a more mature and attractive one.

Timeo, noticing the change of mood in Damien, set about completing the details he knew about me. "Your

Highness will remember that Miss Aromê is the daughter of the Master Perfumer."

"Of course! That's why you love so much to surround yourself with flowers."

"That's right, Your Highness. I love being in your presence. I mean, their presence!" The words escaped my mouth exposing a confession that surprised both me and Damien.

At this, he fixed his gaze on me and I could notice his face softening. Feeling exposed, I added: "That is, a garden is always a good place to think, do you not agree?"

"I guess you're right. Tell me, what does a girl like you think about?"

"Not in drawings and embroidery," I confessed, letting him see that I was not what they would call a conventional girl. By then we were walking between the rows of lavender, followed by Timeo a few steps back. We talked about how much I admired my father and about our early walks in the meadow chasing smells. I said so much that Damien perceived that I have the same passion for perfumes and fragrances.

"A courtesan perfumer, who would have imagined it!"

"The same person who accepted the idea that fairies are the ones who perfume the flowers."

"Touché!" He said, defeated. In that Timeo reminds him that he must return for the coronation ceremony.

"Your father is an honorable man who opened my eyes to the conspiracies against the life of my father and for that, I will be eternally grateful. I wish he and I had seen each other before. My father would still be alive."

At that time, I felt it necessary to show my support, "Your Highness...

"Damien," He said, permitting me to speak to him closely...

"Damien, I cannot imagine how difficult this moment is. If something happened to my father, I do not know what I would do. But one thing is certain, everyone in the kingdom admired the King and that same admiration we feel for his son—that is, for his second son—and I do not doubt that your father knew it too."

On his face, I could see that he was pleased. Although, knowing that this would be the last time I would see him, I had to say everything I had inside. "...and we will miss you when you leave for your new kingdom."

"I certainly had not taken into account what I was giving away."

I had not realized how painful the idea was. Knowing that I was about to burst into tears, I hastened to excuse myself by saying that I should return to my family.

"Come with me. I want you to be at the ceremony."

"Really? I do not know what to say..."

"Say yes!"

"This way Mademoiselle." Said Timeo, telling me where to go.

Our entrance together to the palace did not go unnoticed. Duke Du Virgile renewed his discontent upon learning that I was the daughter of the perfumer. Ever since the death of the King, and the hanging of the physician, the ministers continued with the investigations of what person or persons were involved. Not only to do justice but to preserve the lives of the new kings. Henceforth the Duke was determined to find someone to blame.

The division of the kingdom was also something that he planned on fixing. He wanted the whole kingdom for himself, and he would not tolerate others rising against him, once he had eliminated his nephews. But he needed three things; resources, someone to blame for the death of the King, and to prevent Damien from taking his place in the new kingdom. Seeing the preferential treatment Damien bestowed upon me and my family at the ceremony, he knew exactly what he would do...

The ceremony was celebrated with the presentation of a new shield as a badge for Damien's kingdom. Both brothers were then crowned. A new military order was also selected, pronouncing the territorial divisions and privileges of both monarchs, as well as covenants preventing rivalry between them.

Seeing him crowned King, I felt joy for Damien, knowing that his brother would not deprive him of what his father gave him. But at the same time, on the inside, my heart was fading like a flower in summer, in the heat of the inevitable farewell. In a week, he would leave, taking a part of me with him.

Back at home, I had trouble concentrating. In the greenhouse, Emilien waited with enthusiasm to know what would come out of the new ingredients that he had collected for me in the days that I was attending the palace. "I went deep into the woods for these, you know? We must take advantage of the fact that they are still fresh." And even though I knew he was right, for the first time my enthusiasm was in a limbo. I did not want to admit it, because it was absurd to fall in love with a Prince—that is, a King—and hope to be reciprocated. Emilien insisted on knowing what was happening to me, even though he suspected it...

"Focusing on doing what you like is the best distraction."

"And how do you know?"

"I have been practicing for years."

By telling me this, I could not help feeling deep respect for him, recognizing how valuable he was as a friend. My mother had also noticed a change in me, but she did not push me. There was already a lot of tension in our family, more than I was aware of. One of them was due to my father's certainty that we were in danger. And no wonder, in fact, none of our home affairs went unnoticed. Hidden in the vicinity, men sent by the Duke kept watching us day and night. They wanted to discover our secrets, to seize everything that my father possessed. They also focused their attention on me, to use me as bait for both him and Damien.

Meanwhile, in the palace, the new King Bastier was involved in the affairs of the crown. Duke Du Virgile, well aware of his weakness of character, set in motion his plans...

"There is a matter of concern that the King should know if His Highness wants to begin His reign with the kingdom firmly under His command." He told him in confidence.

"What is it, Duke?"

"It's an idea, rather a suspicion... I might be wrong, but I leave it to the King's decision and wisdom."

"Speak, and choose your words well, making sure they have a foundation."

"Of course my Lord, as you will know, the matter of the attack against His father is not yet resolved. I would hate to think that the perpetrators get away with it... "

"Go on..." Bastier said intrigued.

"I was thinking, is it not the best way to overlook our enemy, to have him close, so much so that he makes us believe he is on our side?"

"I guess you have someone in mind."

"It is not an accusation, rather a feeling that something is not right."

"Explain yourself without further ado!"

"Haven't you wondered how close to the crown the Master Perfumer and all his family have been lately?"

"The perfumer? But it was he who denounced the poisoning of my father."

"Exactly! Is it not by chance that His Majesty was the only one using a fragrance created by him?" That hint seemed likely to Bastier.

"Indeed! Only my father has worn that perfume."

"...and how is it possible that of all those who took care of His Highness, only he in one visit could detect exactly what poison had been used?"

"Someone who is an expert in the field..."

"...or one who has achieved what he intended." The Duke feigned consternation over his brother's death, to confuse Bastier. It was obvious that he had succeeded in casting doubt on him, now he intended to invite him to seek for the evidence.

"Assuming that what you say is true, what gain could he have? He has no chance of assuming the crown."

"Not directly, but how about placing the crown on someone from his family? Did his Majesty not see the daughter of the perfumer accompanying Damien at the coronation ceremony?"

"You're right; I had not seen the connection." Bastier was intrigued by the thought. However, he held a certain doubt...

"But then, why go after Damien if he is King of a small and insignificant place? Why not come for me?"

"Either he chose from the two Kings the most vulnerable one," He said, feeding his ego, "...or helped the one he works for."

"Are you implying that Damien ordered his own father to be killed?"

"Ambition can be a bad counselor, my Lord. And accepting a false kingdom as an amendment, instead of being the successor of all-"

"But the supreme successor is me, for that he would have to eliminate me too."

Making use of false consternation, he made his insinuation clear. "That is what I fear, my Lord. That they are planning something against His Highness, the new King." Bastier was visibly convinced with the possibility. "Of course all this is just a theory."

"A theory worth confirming." Said Bastier convinced and frightened.

"My Lord will understand the importance of keeping the matter in complete discretion since we do not know who else might be involved."

"Of course. The matter has to be handled only between you and me. Do whatever it takes."

"It will be done as the King orders. Ah! One more thing, Your Highness ...The King should not use the perfume of His father."

"Take it and look for someone to have it checked."

Satisfied, Duke Du Virgile put his plan in motion. Five days had passed since the coronation, and Damien was preparing to leave. But there was something he wanted to do before he left. Intrigued by the beautiful courtesan perfumer, he longed to see her and confirm if perhaps what he had perceived on that day was correct. Proposing to invite the perfumer to a meeting in the palace, he wanted to carry the message himself. So accompanied by Timeo, now named captain of his cavalry, they came to our house.

"King Damien!" My mother exclaimed when she received him. "To what do we owe the honor of your presence?"

"I want to have an encounter with the Master Perfumer in the palace as soon as possible."

"It will be an honor. I'll send someone to tell him at the school."

"Of course, only the invitation is for the whole family."

"Thank you, Your Highness. We will be there."

"Speaking of your family, where is the rest?"

My mother, pleased with his particular interest, suspecting that he was asking indirectly for me, followed the current, "My son is back in our lab and Aromê in her greenhouse, next to the gardens."

"May I know your gardens, Madame?"

"Say no more my King, my house is your house."

Dismounting the horse, he went inside the house, to the yard, on the way to the back garden. From there they were told to cross the small bridge that connected an entire valley full of flowers and fruits. The greenhouse was not far away. My mother told him to enter knowing that I would be found there.

It's been a few days since I had found a little goldfinch, whose nest had fallen. Determined to save my little friend, Emilien and I fed him with wild berries and worms. And that was what we were doing when suddenly Damien came in causing Emilien to drop a few dishes in surprise.

"Someone is going to have to go for more wild berries, my little one is hungry again," I said to Emilien, who remained mute.

"Now you're also a bird-enchantress!" I heard a familiar voice say, sending a chill through my body. I turned slowly, fearing it was just my imagination, but it was true, Damien was there, in my greenhouse!

As I bowed, I replied, "I only rescued a helpless little bird, Your Highness."

"Damien." He told me again, resuming his permission to speak to him without protocol.

"Damien, I present you to Emilien, my best and most faithful friend. And partner in experiments."

"Victim is more realistic to say! Your Highness, it is an honor."

"Having a good friend is a rare treasure if I knew anything about that!"

We left the greenhouse and soon found ourselves walking among the flowers.

"Then it is here where the Fairy of Flower creates her magic potions."

"That's right; this is my magical and enchanted forest of flowers and secret ingredients."

"I hope to know some of your experiments or perhaps a perfume made by you."

"Your wish was already granted in advance with the perfume you wear."

He smiled and showed me he was pleased. "Then I'll treasure it even more."

"I cannot deny that I'm surprised to see you here."

"I hope to be a pleasant surprise."

"Without a doubt. Very pleasant!"

"I came to invite you to the palace this afternoon. There's something I want to talk about with your father."

"I did not think it possible to see you again before..."

"Before I leave? On the contrary, I could not leave without coming beforehand."

In that, my mother and brother came to agree on the exact time that we would see each other that afternoon. Damien returned to the palace as we ran to get ready and join our father. At the same time, a messenger from the men who watched us ran to inform the Duke of Damien's visit to our house.

"It's the perfect excuse to justify my next move." Said the Duke before notifying Bastier.

"It is obvious that they are plotting something, and His Highness the King must be extremely careful, watching Damien at every step."

"Deep inside I hoped you were wrong, but now I do not doubt that this is all true. I will accuse him of treason and condemn him to the dungeon!"

"It is a good plan indeed, Your Highness, once we have evidence against him. The King will not want to gain the scrutiny of the people and divide the kingdom."

"The kingdom is already divided."

"And it will be unified again under your command, once we demonstrate Damien's betrayal."

"I'm very lucky to have you as counselor, Duke, you will certainly remain in the high affairs of the crown."

"You cannot imagine how high." Thought the Duke, bowing before Bastier. He then ordered to be informed when the perfumer arrived. In the early hours of the afternoon, already in the palace, we were told to go to the halls of the east, where Damien attended to his affairs. We were received by a delegation of ministers who were part of his royal cabinet. We were given a seat in front of a large semicircular table, where all discerned themes and decisions that were in line with the mandate and management of the new kingdom. Damien was sitting in the center.

The provincial chiefs announced their plans of how they would receive the King on his reconnaissance trip and the road map. Thus, of the three cities chosen to build a palace, Damien would have the last word. Then, talking directly to my father, he asked to be reported on how the affairs of perfumery were handled and of the schools established by his father. Just as he was about to begin, they interrupted him by giving Damien an urgent message. Duke Du Virgile asked to see the King as a matter of urgency to deal with a matter of vital importance. Due to the insistence, Damien granted his permission to enter.

"What is so urgent that you bring, that you cannot wait, Duke?" He asked squarely. Damien had his uncle for a vain and difficult man, who his father always warned him to keep his distance. As he approached he gave both my father and me a hard and arrogant look, which denoted his contempt.

"Your Highness it is nothing serious, pardon if I gave you such an impression. On the contrary, I have been commissioned by your brother the Supreme King Bastier, that His Highness devotes space in his time to attend a banquet."

"A banquet? Is there not an official farewell ceremony scheduled?"

"Yes, Your Highness, but this would be a private one among the Kings. A kind gesture from the King to honor his younger brother."

Disguising his mistrust, Damien accepted before indicating to the Duke that he could withdraw. As he was living, the Duke pretended that he had twisted one foot, requiring a seat. Apologizing for the interruption, he asked them to continue their discussions, promising that he would leave as soon as he felt better.

Taking the floor, my father spoke openly about how much demand there was for placement as students, as well as perfumes and cosmetics. Speaking also of the trade-in ingredients, he explained how active it was with the import and export channels. Damien praised the fact that such a legacy from his father was making significant progress, and explained that he longed to do the same in his portion of the kingdom. So he asked if he and the whole family would be willing to travel and spend time exploring the grounds for the gardens and locations where he could open the first school in his kingdom.

My father would have wished the Duke had not been present when Damien made the proposal. It seemed the best idea he had heard lately and a solution to the danger we were in. My mother and I looked at each other excitedly, for far from the reasons my father was contemplating, we, or at least I, let my imagination fly with the idea of seeing Damien again and perhaps...

"Indicate His Majesty the date and we will be honored to serve him."

"So shall it be. I will send messengers as soon as I determine a place to receive you, and your journey will be at the expense of the crown."

Damien and I exchanged glances, while my father watched the Duke go. Back at home, he entrusted us with great care, for he had or rather knew that the Duke was plotting something. And he was right because what we did not know is that, with the commotion caused by the visit of

Damien in our house, my brother Florian, fearing that something was happening, opened one of the windows of the property where we hid the workshop. Upon seeing him, the Duke's spies immediately reported that they had found the place where the royal perfumes were made. With this and now knowing all the details of sales and marketing, he became convinced that his days of shortages were over.

The banquet between the brothers was a strange encounter, in which Bastier as host played a bad role. Damien did not enjoy it either, he felt questioned by the way the conversations were conducted. Far from a courtesy between relatives, who say goodbye, turned out to be another unpleasant and unnecessary moment.

The day of departure arrived, the caravan of officers and chariots on horseback filled the main streets. People were looking for a place to watch the parade. My father's school was on the main road. There we stopped to see the Royal

Caravan. In the village, they all lamented that Damien had to leave. Most wanted it another way and above all, no one craved it more than me. But I was comforted by the idea that he would send for us. "Three months pass by quickly," I said, calming my anxieties.

Timeo commanded the passage of the Royal Chariot. When they saw Damien the locals threw flowers, and they bid farewell to the King and presented gifts, which were collected by his officers. Once in front of us, Timeo ordered the car to be stopped, allowing my father and me to talk to him. "Long live the King!" They cried, before staying silent in astonishment, at the sight of him approaching me. My father offered a trunk which they put in his carriage. "I'll look forward to the day I see you again." He said, sealing my heart to his.

"I cannot wait any longer," I confessed before handing him a bottle of his perfume and another with mine.

Before he climbed into his carriage, he kissed my hand, placing a locket—engraved with his image—inside. Rumors that I was King Damien's fiancée were whispering everywhere. Emilien did not miss an opportunity to bother me, calling me "Queen Aromê." But I completely ignored him. In the greenhouse, the song of my already-grown goldfinch made me follow with my imagination Damien's caravan. He had been traveling for three days, I imagined him traveling through new places and being greeted with joy. Oh, how I envied those people! Always bearing my locket, I looked at the inscription to feel him close.

That day, when my father returned home, guards surrounded the property, ordering him to surrender to those who sought to arrest him. Demanding to know what he was accused of, he was told that he had poisoned the late King. Duke Du Virgile ordered the guards to confiscate everything we owned and apprehend all members of the family. My father confronted him, allowing my mother to flee. She rushed to the greenhouse to protect me, followed by guards. Men in the service of the Duke broke everything in their path, seeking money and demanding from the servants every object of value. My father, severely beaten, was dragged into the hidden workshop, where the Duke— after finding the royal perfume—claimed to have also found bottles with poison.

"You are nothing but a vulgar thief who uses slander to take possession of what does not belong to you!" My father yelled at him. The Duke slapped him and ordered him to humble himself before him. "That's how you speak to royalty?"

"Royalty? No title can hide the reality: you are a criminal. Everyone knows that you are nothing more than mediocre, a crook who will never become king."

"And who is going to stand in my way, you and your house of gardeners? Or maybe your daughter?"

"Two Kings are above you, and they will crush you."

"Ah yes, the Kings. Damien will not arrive alive to his destination. A pitiful accident will reap his young life. And Bastier, well, Bastier will die in the same circumstances as his father, and I'll find a way to accuse you too. I will destroy your name from among the perfumers, and the rest of your family will smell rotten in the dungeons of the palace." Seeing my brother being caught, my father struggled and managed to throw a bottle of alcohol. The liquid splashed on the face of the Duke, who tripped over lamps and other jars, causing a fire. Fearing for his life he ordered to be taken out of there. When he felt the pain of the burns on his face he used his dagger to kill my father.

Meanwhile, in the greenhouse, my mother came yelling at me to flee. But before I could react a guard grabs me, causing a great confusion of screams and threats. For his part, Emilien, seeing me in danger, threw bottles with the chemicals that provoke the white smoke. This confused the guards, which allowed my mother to free me from them, letting herself be trapped in my place. I tried to go back wanting to help her, but in that some arms grabbed me, forcing me to run through the back door, also ripping the locket from my neck. In the distance, smoke rose in the direction of my house, Emilien made me run holding onto me with strength and ignoring my pleas.

Behind us, we heard the sound of a horse approaching, and before we could react, I was raptured. Didier following my father's instructions rushed to my aid.

"Run!" He shouted to Emilien. "Go after King Damien, he's in danger too, Duke Du Virgile ordered him killed, I'll take care of her."

Chapter 7

My Encounter With Damien

I did not wake up until after three days had passed. Not knowing where I was or what had become of my family. I felt weak and confused, all I could remember were the cries of my mother and guards trying to catch me. What had all this been? Why did the royal guard attack us? Remembering the warnings of my father, I presumed the worst. "Mom, dad?" I groaned for them. Did the Duke do this? Will King Bastier know? Will Damien know? Touching my neck, I looked for the locket only to realize I did not have it. I searched for it in that room I did not recognize, but it was not here. A deep anguish seized me. I felt desolate and lost.

Not far away, I heard voices. Wanting for them to be from my family, I staggered through that strange place to a small living room.

"Miss Aromê, you should not be standing!" a familiar face told me at last. It was Sofi, Didier's wife, who forced me to sit down.

"Where are my parents? Is Florian here? I want to see them."

"You'd better go back to bed until you're better."

Her elusive reply let me know that something was being hidden from me. I began to cry imagining the worst, suddenly my perfect world had collapsed. I had never experienced such a desolation. Sofi tried to calm me down until finally, Didier came to see me.

"Your father knew that Duke Du Virgile was plotting something against him and that it was a matter of time. He commanded me to take care of you and to take your family to safety."

"A safe place you say? Is that where they are now?"

"No, Miss Aromê..."

"No! No! No!" I shouted thinking they were all dead. He insisted I should calm myself down. Didier told me how the Duke had sent spies to watch us until he discovered where the perfumes were made. He said he did not know under what trick he managed to convince King Bastier, and now the royal guard had my mother and brother taken to jail. I asked about my father, he promised to take me to him when I was strong enough.

An hour later, wearing men's clothing I disguised my appearance. The Duke had put a price on my head, so no one should know where I was. "I'm already stronger," I said to Didier with determination. "Take me to my father."

"Are you sure, miss Aromê?"

"I've never been so sure in my life!"

There was a peculiar being there called Shin Shin. An Asian man of small stature and a few words. I was told that he had come with my father on his last trip. He knew a lot of plants and flowers, so he was sent to the place that my father kept secretly, to plant the gardens. My father had sent for him to prepare a trip. He had not said anything to the family, but within his plans was that we would move in a few weeks. Carrying a steaming cup, Shin Shin came up to offer it to me. He spoke with a strong accent and everything he said he repeated twice. "Aromê, Aromê - take, take - strong, strong."

"He wants you to take it," Didier explained. It was a bitter elixir made of herbs and roots, which in a short time renewed my vitality.

We walked up a hill behind the property. In a newly planted garden, an improvised tomb emerged. "Here lies the Master Perfumer" read the inscription newly carved in stone. I allowed myself to cry, expressing how much I loved him. I swore I would do my best to rescue my mother and brother. I also swore I would not let his legacy be lost.

"I love you, father, I will love you forever!"

Standing next to me was the tiny Shin Shin. He had a cage with him; it was my goldfinch, which sang as if he recognized me. He also brought a large basket, with jars and pots from my greenhouse. When I saw them, I remembered the moment when my mother was struggling with the guards for me to flee, and how Emilien snatched me hard. I have to go back, I thought. Everything I needed to save my family was there. And maybe, hopefully, with luck, I'd find my locket too. The next morning, while still dark, I ran to the hill where the Master Perfumer lay.

"I have to do it, Father!" I explained between cries, "I have to rescue them, help me, from wherever you are, let me know that you are with me!" I opened my arms and closed my eyes to connect with him through my memories. With my nose held high, I took a deep breath, catching the scent of the dewy flowers. A delicate breeze circled me as if to embrace me. Deep in my being, I heard his voice: "Be brave and be strong!"

I mounted the horse and ran in the direction of Emilien's house. From there, I could look up the hill where my greenhouse was. Duke Du Virgile had claimed our property as his own, as well as all the benefits of the school of perfumes, and the trade of spices. In the city, all murmured about the death of my father. Among the rumors, those who inclined towards royalty said that he had poisoned the King. However, others intertwined stories of men who helped the Duke to take revenge on the perfumer for having refused to give him the perfume of his brother the King. The latest story had more credibility, knowing full well that the Duke was a mean and envious little man.

Since it was still too soon to know the truth, they speculated what other ruses the Duke had at hand, and what would be the fate of the family held as prisoners. As for me, it was said that I had gone to seek refuge after king Damien, after all, they had seen him treat me with special gallantry. What no one knew was how aware he was of the danger his uncle represented, because of my father. As wise as he was, he told Damien of his suspicions in letters that he hid in the interior of the trunk that he gave as an offering. The letters also asked for his help to protect us when we traveled.

Damien discovered them two days later when he requested that the trunk be opened to store the bottles of perfumes I had given him. By the time Emilien was able to catch up with him, he watched as Damien's soldiers fought with a band of mercenaries attacking them. Emilien saw arrows going through the curtains where the royal carriage was. Taking a torch, he ran around causing a fire, giving rise to the soldiers who protected the car to flee.

Emilien followed them to make sure Damien was still alive. At that, two men on horseback intercepted him. They were Damien and Timeo, dressed in ordinary clothes.

"King!" Exclaimed Emilien exhausted. "I am glad to see you alive!"

"What are you doing here? Where is Aromê?"

"Duke Du Virgile attacked her house then killed the Master Perfumer. Her mother and brother have been taken as prisoners."

"What happened to her, where is Aromê?"

"The guards attacked us while we were in the greenhouse when they took Aromê, her mother attacked the guards. I took hold of Aromê and fled into the woods, until Didier, the perfumer's servant, snatched her from me. He said that he would take care of her and told me to come after you to warn you of the attack, the Duke prepared to kill you."

"Is my brother still alive?

"I wouldn't know, Your Majesty."

"Faithful friend, you can call me Damien! I found more loyalty in you than in my own family. My father warned me well of that viper. I do not doubt that he and no one else is responsible for my father's death. He would do anything to become king. I just hope it's not too late for Bastier. Now let's go back to help Aromê."

Hidden among the gardens near the greenhouse, I snuck up to make sure no one saw me. Then I shuddered as I felt a hand clinging to my foot. It was Shin Shin, who had followed me. "Come, come!" He said, indicating that I should follow him. Once inside, I saw my greenhouse destroyed a second time. Refusing to cry, I searched through the rubble trying to find my locket. Convinced that it too had been lost forever, I went through the baskets where I had my wax traps. They were stuffed hollow balls, some with an herbal extract that caused itching and others with the essence that made the beasts flee. In that, we heard footsteps outside. So, armed with my potions, and with the help of Shin Shin, we snuck away.

We saw the silhouettes of three men who entered the greenhouse through the back door, and then back out.

Hidden in the thickets, Shin Shin and I stood motionless as one of them approached us. He was a few steps away from me. Determined to defend myself, I threw several balls of the itching substance. Also, Shin Shin threw dirt on his face. The man began to scream from the itch and to grunt from the earth in his eyes. When we saw the other two men running in our direction we fled. In that, a familiar voice shouted my name...

"Aromê, wait!"

"Emilien?!"

I stopped at the surprise of seeing him there, at his side ran Timeo in the direction of the one who complained. That's when I saw who it was. It was Damien, who was now pulling off his clothes. Regretfully, I indicated that we should take him to the small stream so he could bathe. In a short time, Shin Shin appeared with some leaves, which he rubbed on his skin, calming the itch.

Crying, unable to contain the accumulation of emotions upon seeing them, I tried to apologize.

"You do not know how sorry I am, I thought you were coming to catch me, Damien, Emilien!" But before I could say more, Damien clung to me in a big hug.

"Aromê, my Fairy of Perfumes!" He kept saying by holding me. "You're okay! You're safe!"

Overwhelmed by that sense of protection, I clung to him with all my strength. His body, despite being wet, impregnated me with a warm sensation of solace. It was not decorous, but I did not want to let go.

"I was so afraid that the same thing happened to you as my father. My father!" I said between sobs. "My family!"

"I know." He said, wiping my tears and stroking my face. "I came as soon as I heard. Emilien not only came to tell me, but he also helped save my life."

Grateful to my faithful friend, I ran to hug him. Then he made me the object of one of his jokes. "We thought of coming to rescue you and look at the whooping you gave King Damien!"

"She's not a helpless little girl!" Timeo exclaimed, helping to dress the King.

"Of course not!" Said Damien with pride. "Her potions defend her very well!"

"Come, come." Shin Shin said, warning us of men approaching. I had to explain to Emilien who he was, to satisfy his curiosity.

Chapter 8

The Rescue

Back at Didier's house, we learned that king Bastier not only remained alive but was still blinded by the Duke's lies. He was convinced that Damien and the Master Perfumer had conspired against his father and now against him to possess the crown. The messengers who returned to the palace to give the news of the attack against Damien were captured, orders were given to also capture the treacherous King. The news spread throughout the colonies, generating disputes between those who were in favor of King Damien and against King Bastier. This same division occurred in the castle among the ministers, some of whom refused to accept the intrigues of the Duke. Thus, the image of king Bastier was weakened, while a secret movement of men set out to find Damien and expose the Duke before it was too late.

Prepared to remove anyone who stood in his way, Duke Du Virgile raised before Bastier suspicion of betrayal of all those who advocated for Damien.

"These opponents are not loyal to my Lord the King. They doubt His word instead of devising how to protect him from what His brother plots."

"I still have a hard time believing that Damien is behind all this. He could have well devised his plan from the moment my father divided the kingdom, and it was not so. I saw him take the order without protest."

"The King must not lose objectivity. The nobility of His heart makes him doubt reality."

"And what is that reality? As the ministers ask, where is the evidence?"

"What more proof than that of spies we catch wanting to enter the palace?"

"Exactly, to leave and return days later pretending that three guards are going to conquer an entire army? What kind of strategy is that? Wasn't it better to attack me from the inside with all his army still here?"

"I admit that it is an ill-conceived plan, my Lord, but it is the result of an incapable mind, blinded by envy. Damien has always hated being in the shadow of his brother. He grew up knowing that unless you disappeared, he would be no more than a secondary title in the kingdom. In his journey, seeing reality, devised the way to return."

"Where is he now?"

"Soon we will know, my Lord; soon we will know!"

"Any news about my mother and my brother?"

"Only that they remain imprisoned in the dungeons, but not for long. If they are accused of treason, they will be condemned to hang," Didier explained, causing me to burst into tears.

"I'm not going to let that happen, I promise," Damien told me. "Timeo and I have a plan."

Drawing a rustic map on a piece of paper, they explained secret passages through which one could enter the palace. Timeo showed the area of the dungeons and the weak points by which we could remove the prisoners. We need someone to come in and open the door to the passage. There is a gap to enter, but It Is very narrow.

"Shin Shin, Shin Shin!" He said volunteering, which we all agreed.

"I'll go too," I announced, determined, "...and do not try to convince me otherwise."

Damien knew he could not stop me. "On the condition that you do not leave my side for one moment."

At dusk, armed and determined, we were about to leave, when Didier arrived with a troop of men. "King Damien, there is someone who wants to see you." It was Sir Charles, one of the late King's closest Ministers. He told him all the slanders that Duke Du Virgile had raised against him, and with which he had deceived Bastier. He also said that he had noticed in him the same symptoms as his father at the beginning of his illness.

"Bastier will die poisoned if we do not do something and soon. Aromê, do you know if there is an antidote?" In that, Shin Shin came carrying a strange jar and herbs in his hand.

"Mix, take - mix, take."

"It seems that our little friend has a solution for everything!" Damien said, pleased.

"One more thing, my King." The minister extended a document wrapped in a piece of leather. In it, the Duke instructed several men to provoke a revolt after the hanging of the prisoners that would be carried out the following day. Stating that the three ministers who were opposing him were to die.

"We caught them as they recruited men in the tavern."

"One moment!" I said, asking to sniff the document. "It's the perfume your father used." I told Damien. "This is why the Duke killed my father; he refused to give him the same perfume that his brother the King used."

"I swear on my father's name that I will avenge both deaths." Taking command before these men he proposed to give the Duke what he intended.

That night, while I was preparing bags with all sorts of wax bombs, my little bird hopped back and forth in the cage. He seemed anxious as if he sensed the danger ahead. Feeding him, I promised him I would come back and celebrate the freedom of my family, by giving him freedom as well. Damien approached me with something in hand, it was my locket.

"I found it near the greenhouse. Didier repaired the broken chain, and this time I want to make sure to put it on your neck."

"I thought that, like my father, I had lost it forever and that I had lost you forever."

"You will never lose me! My heart is perfumed with you my Aromê; and nothing and no one will ever interpose between us."

I lifted my hair allowing him to place the locket. "And I will carry you in my heart forever!"

With a kiss, we seal our oath of love. We held each other as we did in the stream. I did not want time to pass by so I wouldn't have to let go. Him, longing to protect me from all danger, held me tight and tenderly at the same time.

At that moment Timeo and Emilien came to announce that they were all ready.

In the early hours of the morning, when the night is darkest, we slip through the gardens of the palace in the east wing. Damien and Timeo knew the area perfectly. Near the door of the secret passageway, Shin Shin slipped through the small hole, letting us in. We went through the narrow corridors where we were indicated. Arriving at the doors where the first guard was, Emilien and I threw wax balls with a potion that induced sleeping. In a few minutes, the dormant guards were bound and gagged. Our men took their uniforms and assumed their positions. So we advanced to the second guard, where Shin Shin let himself be seen to make them follow him. There was the risk that the trumpet sounded like an alarm. As they chased him down the aisles, one by one the guards were caught and replaced.

It dawned when we finally got to the dungeons. To make sure my mother and Florian were there, I threw balls with perfumed water. Listening to their voices calling my name, I felt overwhelming relief. To the officers, I threw then a ball containing the stinking substance for which my father called me skunk. The guards there rushed to see what it was, and soon they were caught. Damien and Timeo released my family and immediately the three of us were fused in a hug. As they inquired what we were doing, the three court guards of Damien's army, those who had brought the message, were also released. Now all he had to do was find a way to prove the truth to Bastier.

In the middle of the morning, with my mother and Florian already safe, the executioners came in search of the prisoners, who were covered with hoods hiding their faces. Duke Du Virgile, seated at Bastier's right hand was pleased to see that the prisoners were placed in front of the gallows. He covered half of his face with a hood, to hide the burns that the perfumer caused. Next to the King were Sir Charles and the other two ministers whom the Duke intended to eliminate. The guard contained the multitude of courtiers and villagers who gathered to witness the execution. Some shouted calling them traitors, while others called for clemency. Thus anxiety and confrontations arose that would later justify the revolt.

At the hour when the accusations were read and the death sentence was pronounced, the executioners would put our heads on the ropes, when the alarm was given. Our officers and men mingled in the crowd raised their arms, taking Bastier's officers prisoners. Confused, the Duke shouted demanding an explanation. Then Damien, uncovering his face, showed himself to the crowd. He then shouted and ordered everyone loyal to his father the late King and his brother King Bastier to seize Duke Du Virgile and his men.

Altered the Duke gave a cry of alarm, promulgating treason. Then the trumpets were heard, and soldiers from every part of the palace ran to seize us. Emilien and I threw balls with the itchy substance to stop them. Duke Du Virgile fled, leaving Bastier amid the chaos. He entered the corridors in the direction of the towers, surrounded by his guards, but he felt weak, so it was not much that could advance. Knowing where he was going, Damien told me to follow him, running to intercept Bastier and show him the evidence. But I, seeing the Duke flee in another direction, I followed him. Damien kept calling me, but I intended to stop him at all costs. Emilien ran after me and told Damien that he would protect me. Seeing themselves persecuted, Timeo and Damien made their way through the quarrels, until they entered the palace.

When he saw me running after him, the Duke fled into the courtyard where he met me with some dogs. "What do you propose now? To perfume the beasts? You can throw your potions on Damien, but it won't work on me. The same way I got rid of your father, I will now eliminate you."

"You will never get away with it, Damien will show the truth to King Bastier and that will be your end."

"Damien, Bastier? Those two worms will die today crushed under my feet."

"A crook like you will never become king."

When he heard me say the same words as my father, he became engulfed in more anger. "And who's going to stop me, you? Don't you see that in a few moments you'll be dog food?"

At that, I threw the foul-smelling balls in front of the beasts, causing them to retreat. Then I heard the voice of Emilien, who had been captured.

"Run, Aromê," He shouted, wrestling with the soldiers.

"Either you surrender or he dies." Said the Duke. Emilien screamed incessantly for me to flee, but I could not let him die.

The soldiers led King Bastier to secret chambers, setting guard at the entrance to protect him. When he was left alone he got scared at the sound of his brother's voice.

"Bastier, I'm not your enemy."

"Show yourself now!" He ordered frightened.

"Your real enemy is closer to you than you think," Damien said, emerging from behind a curtain.

"That's what the Duke told me when he opened my eyes to your betrayal."

"How can you believe that lying rat, what evidence has he given you against me?"

"You and the Master Perfumer poisoned my father."

"You cannot distinguish the day from night. Don't you realize that by eliminating us all he'll keep the crown? Look at you, look how weak you are! Have I done this? Are not those the same symptoms that our father presented?"

"You have come to kill me; you want to finish me to keep the kingdom. You have always envied me; you have always wanted what was mine."

"If you're still not convinced, maybe this will." Damien passed the document in the leather roll so he could see its contents. "Do you recognize the seal, the signature, and the letters? Do you recognize the perfume that was from our father? That is why the Master Perfumer died, for having refused to give the Duke the perfume of our father the King."

Smelling the scent imprinted on the leather, he recognized the fragrance.

"He told me not to use the perfume of my father, which was where the poison had been put."

"Who now uses the perfume is the one who attacks your life! He is the true traitor!"

In that the Duke burst into the chamber, bringing us, Emilien and me as trophies. "King Bastier, I've caught two of the-" Seeing Damien there and the leather roll in Bastier's hands the Duke muted.

"Duke, may I have one of your gloves?"

"A glove, my King? For what?" He asked, pretending to be confused.

"I order you to give me one of your gloves!" An enraged Bastier screamed, and immediately one of Bastier's guards grabbed the Duke's right arm, forcing him to release me so he may remove his glove. The Duke, offended, resisted, taking it off by himself. Behind me was Emilien still held by the guards. The atmosphere was tense, and although I wanted to run into Damien's arms, I remained motionless. Timeo was in a defensive position ready to protect his King. Bastier took the glove to his nose confirming the perfume. On his hand, I could see the stains caused by the poison and his fallen face.

"Have you dared to use the perfume that was exclusive for my father? That was supposed to be mine as the new King, the same one you said was poisoned!"

"I was just protecting you!"

"And you still dare to keep lying to me? You accused King Damien of treason and attacked his life-"

"He's the real traitor, he wants to kill you and keep the crown, I'm not your enemy, it's him!"

"Our father always warned us of your wickedness, and of how you were consumed by envy." Damien declared, exposing him. "You did not rest until you took him to the grave, you also killed the Master Perfumer and now you want to do the same with us!"

"She, she is to blame for everything," He said, holding me by the arm again. "She and her father wanted to belong to royalty and they seduced Damien with their potions!"

By that time Sir Charles and the other ministers had come in bringing with them prisoners, adding accusations. "These men have confessed to having received payments to kill King Damien and the Perfumer."

"All this is nothing more than a conspiracy, King Bastier. They envy me and my Lord..."

Bastier, opening the leather showed the letter with the signature and the seal of the Duke. "This is your letter, your seal, and your signature. The perfume you coveted that is imprinted in this document also gives you away. But from now on, the only perfume you'll smell of will be that of the stench in the dungeons until the day they hang you on the gallows. I Bastier, the King!"

"The King, the King! Ah! You are not my king, neither of you are! The only one to whom the crown belongs to is me, me!" He shouted, keeping me as his hostage, holding a dagger up to my neck."

"Guards, I am the true king, to whom by right belongs to the throne, I order you to imprison these imposters."

Damien taking out his sword was preparing to defend me, but the Duke shouted to him to retire or he would kill me. In my hand, I grabbed the last ball of wax I brought, which I burst into his face. Falling into his burns, the itching caused him terrible pain, which Damien took advantage of to free me, leaving him and the Duke engaged in close combat. Enraged, the Duke tried to nail the dagger into him, but Damien, being an expert swordsman, struck him, killing him instantly.

"What an irony, in the end, I will die too!" Bastier said sadly. "...and the kingdom will be all yours Damien."

"It does not have to be that way!" He said, looking into his eyes, making him see that he did not want his death.

"There is an antidote, King Bastier, and His Majesty can still be saved," I said, pointing to Shin Shin, who came up to him with the jar and herbs. By combining them he gave them to the King to drink, which Damien consented so that Bastier would trust.

Chapter 9

The Wedding

Days later, as the kingdom was already calm and Bastier's health was restored, a ceremony would be officiated where the King Bastier would honor all those who had defended his kingdom. All the people celebrated the peace and the good treatment that was among the brothers. Many fascinated with stories of romance, also murmured the possibility of announcing the wedding between King Damien and the daughter of the Master Perfumer.

King Bastier, decorated as knights several of the brave men that helped unmask the Duke, among them Emilien. He also ordered that everything the Duke had taken from us is returned. This seemed good to the family, but the private plans of the lovers were to assume the new kingdom together.

The Kings made a pact of peace, pledging not to interfere in the other's affairs unless they allied mutual defense. Thus the will decreed by each King was absolute and indisputable in their respective kingdoms. Honors were paid to the memory of the Master Perfumer, putting his name to the school. Together, my mother, Florian, and I watched with pride as his reputation was restored. After giving public thanks to Damien and me for exposing the

Duke and saving his life, Bastier said he had one more announcement to make.

"What better way to conclude this saga and start my reign than to bring a queen to my throne? Therefore I have decided to marry." Amazed, all who were present were waiting to know the identity of the courtesan or Princess. Until that moment it wasn't known that King Bastier was courting anyone. "...and that is why I choose Perfumer's daughter, as my wife."

After the shock, everyone in the room was silent. Refusing to believe what I had just heard, I looked at Damien, who stood up enraged and confronted his brother.

"What did you say? How dare you choose her?"

"Her courage helped preserve my kingdom, and what better way to honor her than to make her my Queen?"

"Do you not know what I feel for her?"

"Do you challenge my will before the courtiers of my kingdom?"

"I will not let you. You have always wanted capriciously what belongs to me, and in spite of that, I honored you by saving your life. But it stops now! I will never allow you to take away the woman I love." Damien was immediately restrained by the guards, causing both armies to raise weapons ready to face each other.

"She is a courtesan of my kingdom and I have chosen her. I, King Bastier have spoken!" He said sharply.

Fearing the worst, I shouted, "I accept!"

Damien turned to me pleading. "Aromê, don't do it!"

I could not look at him. I advanced to the stands, leaning before King Bastier. "I accept the proposal of my Lord the King. It will be an honor to be his wife." This last thing I said holding in my hand the locket with the badge of Damien. Timeo shouted, ordering the retreat giving a way out to his king. While Damien was leaving, both armies remained in alert formation. I was immediately instructed to stand by Bastier's side.

"Behold, tomorrow at this hour, at this time, we will celebrate the wedding and all the people will meet their new Queen."

It was to be expected that the people applauded with joy as they had done so far. However, not all acclaimed. Since most of them admired Damien, they felt betrayed and disapproved of Bastier's capricious choice. This was just another sign of envy before the happiness of his brother, with which he condemned the couple to suffer eternal separation from each other. Far from being honored, my heart was bleeding with anguish, but I was willing to sacrifice myself a thousand times, if necessary, to preserve the life of my beloved Damien.

The royal army stood guard at my house day and night. King Bastier ordered Damien to be escorted to the borders of his kingdom, to make sure he would not try to prevent the marriage. As Damien's royal chariot advanced through the forest, he and some of his officers changed their royal uniforms and costumes into common dressings, allowing them to be camouflaged among the locals who came to meet him along the way. They intended to return to the palace and prevent the marriage at any cost.

The new morning rose and at home, everyone hurried with the preparations. Giving the finishing touches to my bridal outfit, my mother and I cried bitterly. I tried to comfort myself when they announced that the royal carriage had come for me. Emilien, bringing Didier and Shin Shin, told us about the lands my father had acquired. Extending me a map he pointed out that it remained in an area belonging to Damien's kingdom. "Come, come." Said Shin Shin with a sad face, handing me the cage with my little bird. Taking him into my hands I asked him to be free for me, and to sing promulgating by the heavens that I was marrying one for the love of another.

The carriage advanced and from the air was followed by the little goldfinch. His song attracted others gathering a flock of birds. In the palace, the gardens had been rearranged, forming a long path that led to the chapel where Bastier was waiting for me. Swearing eternal love, I kissed Damien's badge which I hid in my breast. All along with the planters, were the guests who saw me while I walked towards the altar. Their faces were sad; it was obvious that they felt sorry for me. Among them, Damien and Timeo were in disguise, ready to take me away. Walking slowly, halfway down the road, a white cloud began to emerge from my dress. People began to wonder what all this was, while the whole garden turned white. At the same time, an exuberant aroma scattered, causing a momentary ecstasy. Even the officers and Bastier himself were momentarily delighted and stunned by the perfume that seduced them. The arrival of hundreds of birds that soared singing made them contemplate the sky, and by the time they looked back at me, while the fog cleared, they noticed that I had disappeared.

Damien himself was confused while the remains of my clothes were discovered on the floor. It was such a shock and horror that people ran in all directions confused and frightened.

The news ran all over the kingdom, offering a reward for whoever found the missing Princess. They searched for me in every corner of the kingdom; they hadn't found any trace of me or Shin Shin. Bastier made threats of revenge to his brother, sending spies who sniffed in Damien's kingdom, wanting to discover if he knew of my whereabouts. After a few months, threats of a war between the kingdoms were about to break out, the family of the Perfumer, Didier, and Emilien, decided to immigrate to the kingdom of the blue coast, tormented by the rumors and ghost stories that were said about Aromê. Many townspeople and courtiers disappointed by Bastier's explosive and capricious nature also decided to leave. He became a very unpopular king, about whom songs of dismay were written, singing about family betrayal, and how he was abandoned at the altar.

Thus came the legend of a heroine Princess, who, being unable to be with her true love, transformed herself into a perfume, disappearing from the arms of a traitorous King. Thus I became a Princess without having a kingdom, in legend without having died, and in a fable for lovers whose love is forbidden.

It is also said that in the region of Grasse, in the heart of the Kingdom of the Blue Coast, lives a talented courtesan who makes exquisite perfumes. The news reached the ears of the King who extended her an invitation to the palace, to prepare a perfume worthy of royalty...

To Be Continued...

Discover other works by

Elizabeth Espinal

English Version: BETWEEN TWO KINGS

<u>WHAT READERS SAID IN SOCIAL MEDIA:</u>

Laura Ceballos. Eli, I want to tell you that this book contains a fascinating, wonderful story, it contains a message of faith, of hope, of trust in God, of love... wow! Today I reached one of the most anticipated parts, Pam finally lowers her weapons in front of Sean! What a thrill... I have a little left to finish the book... I invite everyone to read each page and enjoy them as I am doing. Eli, what a beautiful gift you have!

Erika Labour. Dear friend, I could not read the book for 2 days, and I spent that time anxious by thinking about what had happened with Sean and Pamela at the mother's house.

I'm excited to see how Pamela is penetrating Sean's impenetrable barrier. Oh, what a thrill! Blessings.

Katiuska Tejada-Riera. When I bought your book I was reading others and I could not start reading it until today ... Well, yesterday, I stayed up until 2 in the morning and I could not detach from the book... I LOVE IT. It is very entertaining and educational regarding the spiritual... I am captivated by the simple language you use and how you keep my attention alive, excited, and desperate for tomorrow night arrives to continue reading... That if I kept awake it. you must... Good job... I am proud of you! (2) Elizabeth my aunt has been glued to the nook with the book since yesterday... No one can take it off... So let me know where they sell it in Santo Domingo because I think she wants a few to give away.

Karla Melo. Hello woman!! I tell you that, I just finished reading our book, because it no longer belongs only to you, but to your readership, to which I have just joined, and I have enjoyed each of the 418 pages. It has it all: good start (catchy!), Captivating climax (along with the twists), excellent descriptive language and way of handling literary figures, as well as a perfect ending and not to mention teaching. In conclusion, I encourage those who have not read it, to buy it in paperback, electronic or whatever, but BUY IT NOW and start to wake up and enjoy it. I feel very proud of you!! Congratulations and we hope very soon the release of the next book that, although it is now yours, will soon belong to us. Greetings and a big hug to the guys!

Aimee de Leon. Today I have nothing but all the bases to congratulate you, dear friend! I have finished reading your book and I must confess that I loved the plot. I was attentive to the events that were unfolding but even more, I liked the teaching that it leaves us, that is the most important thing! I will keep that, and without giving more details I invite you all to read it! Assuring everyone that you will not regret it! Blessings and success !!!

Elizabeth Espinal

I've been writing stories in my mind since I was little. I did it sometimes to complement my lonely existence and sometimes to escape reality. I invented another world in which I took refuge. Every night I added or removed a chapter. But, by not putting pen to paper, I let them get lost in oblivion. I polished my imagination working as a creative director in advertising agencies. Yet writing stories was like a throbbing unfinished business, waiting its turn in my busy life. By 2010, I found myself unemployed, divorced, a mother of two children, and confined due to a health condition. That's when it happened. The need to escape reality was a better idea than falling into depression. That is why I decided to use writing as therapy. Hence my first novel *Entre Dos Reyes* emerged. A mixture of reality and fiction gave birth to a story of romance and faith, between two complex characters that magnetized each other while they sought to defeat one another.

I confess that I credit God with putting resilience in me. I wrote that story because I needed, with all my being, to have some "happy ending" in my complicated life. The audience's reaction made me see that I had something good in me that I could share. "When will you publish the second part?" Many asked me through social media. "Soon," I have answered, while I am evaluating, what Life-Test must occur for me to immerse myself in this job permanently? In 2017, a light bulb went on. Without any planning, I sat down at the computer, ignored everything that was pending, and in less than a week, Aromê emerged. I shared it with my teenage children—who had many other priorities above hearing my story—I was shocked at the miracle that occurred: they wanted to hear it to the end! Really? My kids are actually captivated and paying attention to my story?! And you would probably believe that, as a writer, I have two book worms for children, but it's not like that, at least not my son. If you don't talk to him about music, he doesn't pay attention to you, not even out of courtesy. My daughter does love reading, but the idea of reading in Spanish didn't appeal to her, even though she can.

When they got to the last chapter, they expected the story to have the same happy ending scheme as other mainstream stories. But when they ran into the shock event, that reaction, followed by the level of adrenaline it generated in both of them (both the male and the female), I knew then that establishing myself as a writer was an option for me. This is how this series came about, which I hope many who are like me, are dreamers, hopeless romantics, can enjoy; so they can escape to the magical world of imagination and adventure...

Thanks for joining me!